Seven Little Monkeys

by Joanie Woodward

Text and illustration copyright ©2005 by Joanie Woodward
Second Printing
Book design by Susan A. Bartlett
Book preparation by H. Donald Kroitzsh
All rights reserved
ISBN 978-0-9754676-4-0   US$19.^{95}
Printed in the United States of America

With honor, this book is dedicated to

Charles W. Woodward, my Dad
and
Chuck Woodward, my brother

Namaste

My heartfelt gratitude to:

The Sunlight of the Spirit

My "Muses" who believed in this book to give it another breath of life.

Marietta L.S.

Gaby

Denise Marika

Donna Woody Woodward

Barbara and David Copithorne

Jo-Anne Sbrega and the Children's Museum of Greater Fall River, MA

Jerry Blakeley of SCORE Boston

Lorraine

Jennifer Copley, Regina Raz, Carol Palmer, Carolyn

My beloved Gregory L. Sisson

Patti and Carla Woodward

Bonnie Clancy

and the host of monkey characters:

Christine Sisson, Trevor, Charlie, Colleen, Maureen and Brian Woodward

James Ward and David DeCosta,

the creative forces at Yeoman House Books who believed and made this book a reality,

and Linda Allen for her passion and commitment to this project.

FOR THE READER

These concepts and words are used in this book:

Yoga: the union of mind, body and spirit

Monkey Mind: in Yoga, this means the busy, chattering, over-occupied mind

Deep Belly Breathing: In yoga, it is also known as the "Complete Breath." Inhaling through the nose, one expands the belly as the diaphram draws down allowing the lungs to expand and fill with oxygen. Then, exhaling through the mouth, the diaphram is relaxed and the belly contracts as the lungs expel carbon dioxide. This method of breathing has a relaxing effect on the nervous system, the mind and the entire body. In some eastern languages, the same word means "breath" and "spirit."

OM: (a Sanskrit word) and ॐ (a Sanskrit symbol) means "unity for all"

Yogi: a male who practices Yoga

Yogini: a female who practices Yoga

Namaste: a Sanskrit concept that means "to honor and see the best in all"

COLORS
The monkey and background color on each page is a reference to the awareness of the seven chakras, which are equivalent to the human endocrine system — the energy regulators of the body.

7 little monkeys jumping in my head.

They were raising quite a ruckus
and I couldn't get to bed.

Daddy called the yogi and the yogi said:

If you have monkeys in your head,
And other woeful woes,
You must breathe deeply, it is said,
down to your very toes!

Breathe in slowly, through your nose
Until it fills your belly,
Then let it out slowly through your mouth
and with it goes
those monkeys – Oh so silly!

 Inhale... Exhale... and go to bed!

6 little monkeys jumping in my head.

They were fussin' and fightin'
and I couldn't get to bed.

Mommy called the yogini and the yogini said;

Take a deep belly breath

and go to bed.

5 little monkeys jumping in my head.

They were acting downright silly

and I couldn't get to bed.

Daddy called the yogi and the yogi said:

Take a deep belly breath

Inhale... Exhale...

and go to bed!

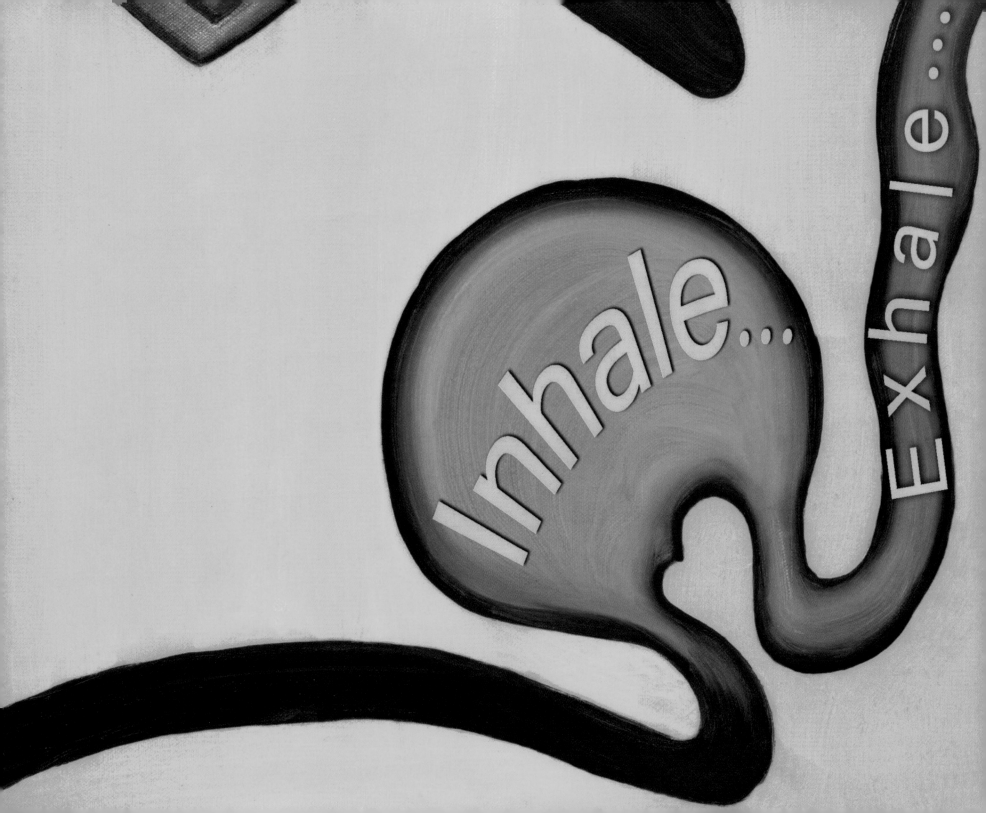

4 little monkeys jumping in my head.

They were feeling mighty frightened and I couldn't get to bed.

Mommy called the yogini and the yogini said;

Take a deep belly breath

and go to bed.

3 little monkeys jumping in my head.

They were angry about something and I couldn't get to bed.

Daddy called the yogi and the yogi said:

Take a deep belly breath

Inhale... Exhale...

and go to bed.

2 little monkeys jumping in my head.

They wanted so to cuddle
and I couldn't get to bed.

Mommy called the yogini and the yogini said:

Take a deep belly breath

and go to bed.

1 little monkey jumping in my head.

He didn't have his friends around
and I couldn't get to bed.

Daddy called the yogi and the yogi said:

Take a deep belly breath

Inhale ... Exhale ...   and go to bed.

Now, at last, there are no more monkeys
jumping in my head.

When I practice deep belly breathing
I can finally GO TO BED!

Namaste

What are the monkeys in YOUR head saying?

What are the monkeys in YOUR head saying?